PINKY BLOOM

AND THE

CASE OF THE MISSING KIDDUSH CUP

JUDY PRESS

ILLUSTRATED BY ERICA-JANE WATERS

KAR-BEN
PUBLISHING

KAR-BEN PUBLISHING
A division of Lerner Publishing Group, Inc.
241 First Avenue North
Minneapolis, MN 55401 USA
1-800-4-KARBEN

Website address: www.karben.com

Main body text set in Bembo Std regular 12.5/17.
Typeface provided by Monotype Typography.

Library of Congress Cataloging-in-Publication Data

Names: Press, Judy, 1944– author.
Title: The case of the missing kiddush cup / by Judy Press.
Description: Minneapolis : Kar-Ben Publishing, [2018] | Series: Pinky Bloom |
    Summary: While investigating suspicious happenings at her friend's parents'
    Chinese restaurant, Brooklyn's greatest detective, fourth grader Penina "Pinky"
    Bloom, solves the mystery of recently stolen artifacts from the Jewish Museum.
Identifiers: LCCN 2017041123 (print) | LCCN 2017013151 (ebook) |
    ISBN 9781541542341 (th : alk. paper) | ISBN 9781541500174 (eb pdf) |
    ISBN 9781541500167 (pb : alk. paper)
Subjects: | CYAC: Mystery and detective stories. | Restaurants—Fiction. |
    Sabotage—Fiction. | Stealing—Fiction. | Jews—United States—Fiction.
Classification: LCC PZ7.P921927 (print) | LCC PZ7.P921927 Cas 2018 (ebook) |
    DDC [Fic]—dc23

LC record available at https://lccn.loc.gov/2017013151

Manufactured in China
1-50727-50121-5/20/2021

0122/B1840/A8

For my mother, Esther Abraham
—J.P.

Chapter One

On Sunday morning, I, Penina "Pinky" Bloom, Brooklyn's greatest kid detective, was lying in bed thinking of ways to get rid of my little brother.

I could have slept late, but someone set my alarm clock to go off at 7:00 a.m.

Avi had been in my room last night, so he was the prime suspect! He's officially the most annoying and sneaky second grader I've ever met.

I couldn't fall back to sleep, so I got dressed and went to the kitchen. My cat, D.J., was prowling around on the counter. He's named for Derek Jeter, the greatest

Yankee ever to play shortstop. I'm in the fourth grade at Ohav Shalom Day School and play catcher on the girls' softball team. Last year our team went to the playoffs and almost beat B'nai Israel's girls' team in the first round.

I was in the middle of pouring myself a glass of orange juice with one hand and petting D.J. with the other when I heard a knock on the front door.

Mom, Dad, and Avi were still asleep, so I ran to see who was there.

"Who is it?" I whispered, standing on tiptoes and squinting through the peephole.

"Open up, Pinky. It's me, Lucy." Lucy Chang, my best friend, lives two floors below me.

I slipped off the chain and opened the door. "Lucy, what are you doing up so early?"

"My mom and dad are arguing, so I thought I'd see if you were awake."

Lucy's parents own the Lotus Blossom Kosher Chinese Restaurant. It opened just a few weeks ago. I wondered if Mr. and Mrs. Chang were fighting about something related to the restaurant, but I figured it would be rude to ask. So I just led Lucy to the kitchen and found the box of cookies my mother had hidden in the back of a cabinet. "Let's have breakfast," I said, handing Lucy a cookie.

Lucy and I sat down at the kitchen table. "There's trouble in the restaurant," she told me. "The chef says he hears weird noises, and the smoke alarm goes off for no reason."

I shoved a cookie in my mouth. "Maybe the place is haunted," I said with my mouth full. "Brooklyn has lots of ghosts."

"But there's more, Pinky! The fortune cookies have really bad fortunes, and customers are so mad they've started eating at the Happy Hunan Restaurant instead."

"What are your parents going to do?" I asked.

"My dad said he might have to sell the restaurant, and then we'd move to a faraway place, like Queens."

That news was worse than when the dentist told my mom I needed braces. I took a swig of juice. "What do your parents think is going on?"

"My dad thinks someone gave the restaurant the evil eye. Pinky, you're Brooklyn's greatest kid detective. You've got to help us."

Evil eyes are a little out of my league, but Lucy is my best friend, and she lets me borrow her pink hoodie with the sparkles on the back.

I shoved another cookie in my mouth. "Okay," I said. "I'll take the case!"

Chapter Two

I grabbed a pencil and a notebook. Across the top of the page I wrote *CASE #2, THE SUSPECTS*.

Case #1 was when I found my cousin Rachel's retainer. Her dog had buried it in their backyard.

"Lucy, let's start with the people who work in the restaurant," I said, using my best detective voice.

"Well, there's Mrs. Wong. Her job is to greet the customers."

I wrote down Mrs. Wong's name. "Who else?"

"Mr. Wong. He's married to Mrs. Wong. He's the chef, and he uses a giant cleaver to chop food."

I made a note next to Mr. Wong's name: *Caution: May be armed and dangerous!*

"Anyone else work in the restaurant?"

"My dad just hired a new waiter because the old one got spooked and quit. His name is Joe."

Before I had a chance to ask Lucy any more questions, my mom and Avi walked into the kitchen.

Avi pointed to Lucy. "It's too early for company," he whined. "Why is she here?"

He was right about it being too early. But if it weren't for him, I'd still be asleep.

I glared at my brother. "Avi, you set my alarm clock wrong last night, and don't say you didn't."

"It wasn't me!" he protested. "Mom, tell her!"

"Settle down, you two," said Mom. "And good morning, Lucy. Can I get you anything?" She eyed the open box of cookies in front of me.

"Sorry to surprise you like this, Mrs. Bloom," said Lucy. "Avi's not wrong about it being pretty early to have visitors."

"That's all right," Mom assured her. "In fact, speaking of visitors, I have some good news. Grandma Phyllis called last night to say she's coming to stay with us for a couple of days."

This didn't totally qualify as good news, in my opinion. I love Grandma Phyllis, but she's a neat freak. The last time she was here she made me take my dirty clothes out from under my bed and put them in the hamper.

"Why's she coming?" I asked, grabbing another cookie before Mom could put the box away.

"There's an exhibit at the Jewish Museum that she wants to see." My class had gone to the museum on a field trip earlier this year. My favorite part was the store where they sold mezuzahs made from Legos.

"What's the exhibit?" I asked.

"It's a collection of ancient Jewish artifacts, including a gold Kiddush cup from Rome."

An old Kiddush cup didn't sound all that exciting to me. We use Great-Grandma Bloom's Kiddush cup on Shabbat and Jewish holidays. She brought it with her from the old country. Maybe she didn't know you could buy a new one right here in Brooklyn?

Suddenly I had a worrying thought. "Where's Grandma Phyllis sleeping?"

"She can sleep in Avi's room," Mom said. "And he'll move into your room."

Sharing my room with Avi is worse than eating brussels sprouts. I groaned. My day had started out bad and had just gotten worse. If I was going to concentrate on solving Lucy's case, I would need to find a way to keep my brother from distracting me!

Chapter Three

Every Sunday night we eat dinner out. Today I picked the Lotus Blossom Kosher Chinese Restaurant, so I could see for myself what was going on.

"Ah, Bloom family. Party of four," Mrs. Wong said when we arrived at the restaurant. "Welcome to everyone. Just a few minutes, please."

I looked around the entryway. On the walls were pictures of China and Israel. I've never been to Israel, but my dad's cousin Elia lives there, and Dad says one day we'll go visit her.

Along one wall was a table with a computer

and phone where Mrs. Wong took orders, and in the corner of the room was a fish tank sitting on a long table.

Avi made a beeline for the fish tank. "Wow," he said, with his nose pressed up against the glass. "Look at that . . ."

Mrs. Wong rushed over to Avi. "This is for you," she said, handing him a tiny paper umbrella. "See, it opens and closes. More fun than a fish tank."

"Table's ready," Mrs. Wong said. "Come with me."

We followed her into the dining room, where we had our choice of tables since most of them were empty. Lucy had been right when she said business was bad.

Mrs. Wong handed us our menus. "Your waiter will be here soon," she said. "His name is Joe."

Avi sat down at the table. He grabbed his chopsticks and put them under his upper lip.

"Arf, arf," he barked, flapping his hands like a seal.

Mom and Dad laughed, but I pretended Avi was some random kid who'd sat down next to us by mistake.

Suddenly the waiter appeared. "You guys ready to order?" he growled.

I looked up at Joe the Waiter. He had shifty eyes and hair slicked back with so much grease you could fry a latke on his head.

I went first. "I'll have the moo goo gai pan," I said proudly. Those are the only Cantonese words I know, but Lucy promised she'd teach me a few more.

Joe the Waiter took out a pen and pad of paper. "Moo goo gai, what?" he said, shaking his head. "How do you spell that?"

I handed him my menu so he could see what I had ordered. Then it was Avi's turn. "I want fried rice," he said. "And I can even spell it backwards— *d-e-i-r-f e-c-i-r.*"

When our dinner finally arrived, Joe the Waiter put my food in front of Avi and mixed up my parents' orders.

I pulled out my notebook. Next to Joe the Waiter's name I wrote, *Something's not kosher.*

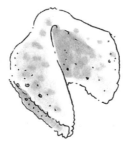

Chapter Four

After we finished eating, I got up from the table and announced, "I'm going to the bathroom."

Avi jumped up out of his seat. "I'm going too," he said.

I was planning on doing some snooping and didn't want my brother tagging along. "Go by yourself, Avi," I hissed at him as we both moved away from the table.

"Pinky, I know you're being a detective, but I can be your helper."

"I don't need your help," I insisted. "We'll meet back at the table."

Avi sighed and headed to the restroom while I took a quick detour to the restaurant's kitchen.

I stuck my head in the doorway. "Excuse me," I called out. "Can you please tell me where the girls' bathroom is?"

A guy in a white chef's coat was busy attacking a carrot with his cleaver.

"Can't you see this is the kitchen?" he yelled, holding the cleaver midair. "The bathroom's down the hall." Chef Wong reminded me of a knife thrower in the circus, and I was hoping he wouldn't use me as part of his act.

A gigantic frying pan was on the stove. It could easily have doubled as a flying saucer.

Along another wall was an oversize refrigerator, and next to that was a door that I guessed led to the alleyway behind the restaurant.

Chef Wong was getting tired of my visit. "Get lost, kid," he said. "Or I'll turn you into chop suey!"

I dashed out of the kitchen and made a brief stop at the restroom before heading back to our table.

Joe the Waiter was clearing off our dishes. "Do you want to take these home?" he asked Avi, eyeing the pile of leftover vegetables sitting on his plate.

Before Avi could protest, my mom told Joe to

put everything in a takeout container. "He'll eat them later," she said. "It's a shame to waste food."

Joe the Waiter dropped a pile of cellophane-wrapped fortune cookies in the middle of our table. Avi reached over and grabbed his first.

"*Fast-food alert. You're a few fries short of a happy meal*," he read out loud. "Hey, that's not true!"

Dad put on his glasses. "Mine says, *Shut your trap. Your teeth are brighter than you are.*"

Next, Mom read her fortune. "*Take more naps. Your beauty sleep is not working.* Wow. Good thing we ate already, or I would've lost my appetite from reading this."

I was beginning to see why the restaurant was losing so many customers.

"Wait, I have to read mine," I said. "*Boo-hoo! A face like yours makes a ghost scream.*"

Avi laughed hysterically, but I didn't think it was so funny.

"Whoever made these fortunes must have flunked out of fortune cookie school," said Avi.

And then graduated from villain school, I thought. These fortunes were too terrible to be an accident. Someone must've written them like this on purpose to sabotage the restaurant. But who would do that?

I stuffed the little white papers with the fortunes into my pocket.

They were crime scene evidence, and I didn't want to leave them behind!

Chapter Five

Mrs. Wong rushed over to our table when she saw us getting ready to leave.

"Family's not happy?" she asked, looking around at our long faces. "Was the food not good tonight?"

"It wasn't the food," my dad offered. "It was the fortunes in the fortune cookies. They were a little hard to swallow!"

"Sorry, Mr. Bloom. Many customers complain. Bad fortunes are bad for business."

"What about the fortune cookie company?" Dad asked. "Did you say something to them?"

"The company said no guarantees on fortunes, only cookies."

As we got up and headed toward the door, I saw that Avi had left his takeout container on the table. I grabbed it and took it with me.

We walked through the restaurant and were almost to the front door when my mom paused.

"Look, that's Mr. Federman!" she said, pointing to a man sitting at a table by himself. "He's the head of special exhibitions at the Jewish Museum."

I looked over at Mr. Federman and suddenly saw something small and furry scurry across the floor.

"Look, a mouse!" I yelled. "It ran under Mr. Federman's table."

Avi immediately dropped down on his hands and knees. He crawled toward the table just as Joe the Waiter walked by carrying a tray of food.

The tray went flying as he tripped over Avi, and a pile of Double Happiness landed in Mr. Federman's lap.

I put Avi's takeout container down on the table and was about to grab hold of him when an alarm went off.

Chef Wong ran out of the kitchen waving his arms and yelling something about the smoke detector.

"Leave the restaurant, now," Mrs. Wong shouted. "I have to call the fire department."

Two takeout containers were on Mr. Federman's table. I figured one was his leftover dinner, and the other was Avi's.

I grabbed Avi's container and followed my family out the door. We were halfway down the street when we heard the roar of fire engines.

Lucy's dad might be right. It certainly seemed as if someone had given the Lotus Blossom Kosher Chinese Restaurant the evil eye!

Chapter Six

When we got home, Avi told me to put his leftover food in the back of the refrigerator, so Mom wouldn't find it. Then he got ready to move into my room, since Grandma Phyllis would be here later tonight.

Avi showed up at my door holding a bobblehead doll from a Yankees baseball game, a book about sharks, and his dead bug collection.

"Yuck, why is your room all pink?" he said, looking around.

"Take all that stuff back to your own room," I told him sternly.

Just then Mom stuck her head in the doorway. "How are you two getting along?" she chimed.

"I don't want Avi in my room. And besides, his feet smell."

"It's only for a few days, Pinky. I'm sure you two will survive."

I was about to tell her she was wrong when the doorbell rang. Avi and I both raced through the living room to answer it.

Dad was talking on his phone but lowered it long enough to say, "Slow down, you two. Whoever's there can wait a minute."

Avi got to the door first. He left the chain on and opened it a crack.

"Let me in," Lucy said. "Your sister and I have important business to discuss."

Avi released the chain and opened the door. Then Lucy and I dashed down the hall to my room.

"Pinky, what happened when you went to the restaurant?" she asked.

I reached inside my pocket and pulled out the slips of paper from the fortune cookies. "Here, take a look at these. I kept them as evidence."

"Wow, it's no wonder customers aren't coming back," Lucy said after she finished reading our fortunes.

"We have to find out who's baking the cookies," I said. "Then we'll know who's writing the fortunes."

"That's easy, Pinky! It's the Rezam Fortune Cookie Company. I saw their name on a box in the restaurant's kitchen."

"That's a good start. Wait here, I'll look them up online." I ran to the living room to ask Dad if I could use the computer.

Avi was already out there with Dad. "Important announcement!" my brother declared. "I might be moving back into my own room."

"Why's that?" I asked, trying not to sound too excited.

"Grandma Phyllis just called," Dad explained. "She just saw on the news that there was a burglary at the Jewish Museum—"

"Some stuff got stolen from the exhibit Grandma Phyllis wants to see," Avi broke in. "That really old Kiddush cup and something else . . ."

"A Torah pointer," said Dad. "The exhibit's temporarily closed until the cup can be located, so Grandma Phyllis might not come to visit."

I felt bad about the burglary and Grandma Phyllis not coming, but I was happy to get my room back. "Go get your stuff out of my room,

Avi!" I ordered him. Then I asked Dad for some computer time.

Five minutes later, I was back in my room with Lucy. "I can't find anything about that fortune cookie company online! Can you ask your parents where the company is and how they heard about it?"

"Sure. But what about the other stuff that's been happening at the restaurant?"

"Well, so far we have three suspects: the Wongs and Joe the Waiter."

"But why would any of them try to cause trouble for the restaurant when their jobs depend on it?"

"Well, maybe they don't actually *like* their jobs. Chef Wong isn't exactly cheerful. He threatened to turn me into chop suey. And Joe the Waiter sure doesn't seem like he cares much about being a good waiter. He messed up all our orders—and he spilled food all over a guy from the Jewish Museum and didn't even apologize."

"Mr. Federman? Oh no. My mom told me he eats at the restaurant all the time," Lucy said. "I hope we don't lose one of our most loyal customers."

"Hmm," I said. "If he eats there a lot, maybe he's seen something that can help us crack the case. Let's talk to him next time he comes back."

"If he comes back," Lucy said glumly. "Pinky, what's next? Am I going to have to move to Queens?"

"Don't worry, Lucy—you've got me, Pinky Bloom, Brooklyn's greatest kid detective, on the case." I tried to sound positive, but this was turning out to be a lot tougher than finding Rachel's retainer.

It was time to pay a visit to Brooklyn's greatest psychic!

Chapter Seven

Everyone in my neighborhood knows Madame Olga. She works out of a storefront a block away from my home. A sign in her window says *Madame Olga, Spiritual Advisor and Psychic to Famous People.*

Once when she was babysitting Avi and me (that's her job when she isn't being psychic), I asked her which famous people got their fortunes read.

"It's top secret, Pinky," she told me. "But I can give you a hint."

Then she wrote the initials *D.J.* on a scrap of paper and showed it to me.

"No way!" I shouted. "Was he really here?"

"I cannot say, darling. But you are the detective, so you must figure it out!"

On Friday morning Mom gave me permission to visit Madame Olga after school. "Take your brother with you," she said. "I have to do some shopping for Shabbat."

That afternoon I waited for Avi outside the entrance to Ohav Shalom. The boys' and girls' classes are separate, so we don't see each other during the school day.

"Over here, Avi!" I shouted when I spotted him leaving the building with a pack of boys.

He jogged over to me. "Pinky, we have to go straight home," he declared. "Moshe is coming over and we're shooting hoops in the playground."

"Great, but first we have to stop at Madame Olga's."

"I don't want to go there! I want to go home."

I had to think of something quickly, before Avi had a meltdown. "Look, if you come with me to Madame Olga's you can play with her cat."

Madame Olga had found a stray cat in an alleyway behind her building. She named it Oy Vey because that's what she yelled when the cat gave birth to four kittens.

"No way, I'm not going!" Avi insisted, stomping his foot. But I knew Avi loved anything with four legs and a tail. "Oy Vey just had kittens," I offered slyly.

Avi sighed. "Okay, I'll go. But only if we stop by Mazer's Bakery, and you buy me a cookie."

"Okay, fine." Mazer's Bakery is just two blocks from Madame Olga's, next door to the Lotus Blossom Kosher Chinese Restaurant. And I figured I had enough money left over from lunch to buy a cookie.

When we got to the bakery, Mrs. Mazer was behind the counter.

"Nu?" she said, tapping her fingers on the glass. "You think I have all day to stand here until you decide?"

Avi spoke up first. "I want a black-and-white cookie, please," he said.

Mrs. Mazer wrapped up the cookie. "That'll be a dollar. And don't give me all pennies. I have enough of them."

I fished my nickels and dimes out of my jacket pocket and laid them on the counter.

Mrs. Mazer counted the coins. "It's not enough. You're a quarter short."

I dug into my other pocket and came up with three acorns and a ticket stub from the Yankees baseball game we'd gone to over the summer.

Suddenly an arm reached over my shoulder and plunked a quarter down on the counter.

I spun around and saw that it was Joe the Waiter!

"Uh—thanks," I stuttered. "That was really nice of you."

"No problem," he said. "And don't forget your cookie."

I took the bag from Mrs. Mazer, and we hurried out of the bakery.

On the way to Madame Olga's, I stopped to tie my shoelace. I looked back and saw someone standing about half a block behind us. His face was hidden by the shadows of a building, but I could tell he was staring at us.

"Walk faster," I told Avi. "I think we're being followed!"

Chapter Eight

A handwritten sign was posted on Madame Olga's door: *The Psychic Is In. Please Knock. I Might Be Taking My Nap.*

I knocked softly and waited a few seconds. When there was no answer, I knocked again.

"I'm coming, I'm coming," I heard her say. "Who's in such a rush they can't wait for a person to answer the door?"

The door opened a crack, and Madame Olga peered out. "Oh, it's you, Pinky. I see you brought Avi. Come in, bubeleh."

Madame Olga was dressed in a long, flowery skirt. Hanging from a chain around her neck was a hamesh hand to ward off the evil eye.

We walked down a narrow hallway and turned into the small living room where Oy Vey was nestled on an overstuffed couch nursing her four kittens. In the center of the room was a wooden table with the glass globe that Madame Olga used to tell her fortunes.

Avi walked over to the couch—quietly, so he wouldn't disturb Oy Vey and her kittens.

"Sit, Pinky darling," Madame Olga said, pulling up a chair for me. "Do you want something to eat? I just made a nice coffee cake. Better than what you'd find at Mazer's Bakery, and she has the nerve to charge eight dollars for a babka."

"I'm fine, thanks," I said. "I came here because I need your help."

Madame Olga put her hand over her heart. "Oy, boy trouble already?"

Avi blurted out, "She likes Noah, but he has a girlfriend."

"Mind your business," I shot back. "And anyway, I don't like boys."

"Well then, what's the matter?" Madame Olga asked gently. "I want to help if I can."

I took in a deep breath. "The problem is my best friend, Lucy. She might move away because her family's restaurant is haunted."

I told Madame Olga about the false alarms and how we saw a mouse in the restaurant.

"Nu, it's not the only restaurant in Brooklyn with mice," she said with a shrug. "Tell me more."

I pulled out the slips of paper with our fortunes. "These were in our cookies."

"These fortunes are enough to give a person heartburn! So who else was in the restaurant that night?"

"There was Mrs. Wong, the hostess, and her husband, the chef. And then Joe the Waiter and Mr. Federman."

"Federman? I know him—charming man. Didn't I see that his museum got robbed last week? Such a shame—those gonifs, those thieves, stole a gold Kiddush cup from hundreds of years ago . . ."

"There was one more person in the restaurant," Avi piped up.

I spun around in my seat. "No, there wasn't!"

"You're wrong, Pinky. I saw a lady with a hat and sunglasses when I went to the bathroom."

"Why didn't you say so?"

"I just did!" Avi shouted.

"Children, children," Madame Olga scolded. "Avi, darling, please tell us about this lady."

"She was carrying a little cage," he said. "It looked a lot like the one my friend Moshe has for his hamster."

I pulled out my notebook and added her to my list of suspects.

My detective brain was telling me that this Hat Lady was up to no good!

Chapter Nine

"What else did you see in the restaurant, Avi?" I asked my star witness as sweetly as possible.

"What's it worth, Pinky? And you'd better make it good."

I quickly offered him two lollipops, a chocolate candy bar, and the use of my new catcher's mitt. All good detectives know there's nothing like a bribe to get a person talking. And it worked.

Avi handed me a scrap of crumpled paper. "The Hat Lady dropped this," he explained. "It happened just as I came out of the bathroom, but by the time I

picked up the paper to give it back to her, she was gone."

I handed the paper to Madame Olga.

She put on her glasses. "This looks like a piece of some kind of order form," she said. "It says here, *Six pumpernickel, nine seeded rye bread, and two dozen rolls.* There's also a phone number with a Brooklyn area code."

"Okay, so we have an order for bread and a phone number," I said. "What do we do now?"

"Trust me, bubeleh—now we consult with the higher powers."

I glanced over at the crystal ball. Hey, I'll try anything, even if it means gazing into a matzo ball!

"Not the ball, Pinky," Madame Olga said. "That's for the tourists."

I watched as she reached under the table and pulled out her laptop computer. "Here's what we need, darlings!"

Avi and I watched as Madame Olga typed in the phone number on the paper. The results of her search popped up a second later.

"Whose number is it?" Avi asked.

"It belongs to the Seaside Cafe." Madame Olga pointed to the top search result. "It's a restaurant inside the New York Aquarium. So we make a visit and find out what kind of monkey business this Hat Lady is up to."

Chapter Ten

Avi and I got home from Madame Olga's before sunset, just in time for Shabbat.

Mom had set the dining room table with her good dishes. "Lucy is joining us for Shabbat dinner," she informed me.

That was good news. I was anxious to catch Lucy up on everything I had learned at Madame Olga's and see if she'd found out anything new.

Mom was about to light the Shabbat candles when there was a knock on the front door and in walked Grandma Phyllis. "Shabbat shalom!" she cried. "I decided to come after all!"

I was happy to see Grandma Phyllis, but judging by the looks of her overstuffed bag, she was planning to stay a long time.

It was time to light the candles. "*Baruch Atah, Adonai, Eloheinu, Melech Haolam, asher kid'shanu b'mitzvotav, v'tzivanu l'hadlik ner shel Shabbat*," Mom chanted.

Dad lifted up Great-Grandma Bloom's Kiddush cup and blessed the wine: "*Baruch Atah, Adonai, Eloheinu, Melech Haolam, borei p'ri hagafen.*"

Avi and I drank grape juice as he touched our heads and said a blessing for children.

Next, he lifted the challah cover and made Ha Motzi over the bread: "*Baruch Atah, Adonai, Eloheinu, Melech Haolam, Hamotzi lechem min haaretz.*"

Grandma Phyllis passed around pieces of challah sprinkled with salt.

"I guess you heard about the thefts at the Jewish Museum?" she said. "A Kiddush cup and a Torah pointer went missing from the special exhibit."

"Why would anyone want to steal those things?" Lucy asked.

"Well, they're very valuable," Dad explained. "They're sacred, one-of-a-kind artifacts from many centuries ago and can never be replaced. And I'm sure a thief could sell them on the black market for a lot of money."

At the end of the meal Lucy thanked everyone, and the two of us raced down the hall to my room. "I haven't had a chance to ask my parents about the fortune cookie company," she said. "They've been so busy with work, and when they're not working they don't want to talk about the restaurant. Do *you* have any good leads, Pinky?"

I told her about the Hat Lady. "She was carrying some sort of cage, so I think she might've brought a mouse into the restaurant."

Lucy gasped and then frowned in concentration. "So how do we track her down?"

"Avi found a slip of paper she dropped. It was a bread order from a restaurant at the New York Aquarium. Which means the Hat Lady has some kind of connection to a place that sells baked goods. I'm betting it's the same company that makes your fortune cookies! And someone at the aquarium's restaurant might be able to tell us about the Hat Lady."

Lucy's eyes lit up. "Let's go there tomorrow! It's Saturday."

"It's Shabbat tomorrow, so we'll have to go Sunday. Madame Olga said she'll go with us too."

Suddenly Avi barged into my room. "Hello, I'm moving in now," he announced. "Pinky, can you give me a hand?"

Oh no, my worst nightmare had come true!

Chapter Eleven

Sunday morning I was getting ready to meet Madame Olga at the subway station for our trip to the New York Aquarium.

"I'm going with you, Pinky Brace-Face," Avi told me firmly. "And you can't stop me."

"No, you're not, Avi Know-It-All. I'm working on a case and it doesn't include you."

Avi stomped his foot. "Yes I am, Mom said so."

This called for desperate measures. "I bet you didn't know that the sharks in the aquarium can swallow a kid your size in one bite," I said.

"I'm not afraid of sharks, Pinky," Avi assured me smugly.

"They also have giant octopuses that wrap their arms around second graders and squeeze the guts out of them."

Avi shrugged his shoulders. "I can spell *octopus* backwards," he said. "*S-u-p-o-t-c-o!*"

"That's so annoying, Avi. And you're still not going with us."

Just then Mom stepped into the room. "Pinky, Grandma Phyllis and I are leaving to go shopping. You can take Avi with you to the aquarium."

"Can't he stay with Dad?"

"Dad's going to the bagel breakfast at the synagogue. I checked with Madame Olga, and she said she'd love to have Avi come along."

It looked as if I'd lost this round. I told Avi to go back to his room and get his things. "Only bring the stuff you need," I said.

"I'm bringing my Cub Scout Manual and hand sanitizer. Grandma Phyllis told me I have to use it after I touch a shark."

"Whatever, Avi," I said, throwing a pair of binoculars and a wrapped-up slice of challah into my backpack. The binoculars were to see things far away, and the challah was because detective work makes me hungry.

When we were ready, Avi and I headed down to Lucy's floor. Lucy was waiting for us at the door to her apartment. "I'm bringing my good-luck charm. It's a tiny dog made out of jade."

"I'm wearing a good-luck necklace too!" I said. I showed her the necklace Grandma Phyllis had given me for my last birthday. It was shaped like the word *chai* for good luck.

"I still haven't been able to find out more about the fortune cookie company," Lucy added apologetically. "So I really hope we get some clues today!"

I nodded. "We'd better get going. Madame Olga's waiting for us at the train station."

Lucy and I walked fast, but Avi lagged behind. "Hurry up or we'll miss our train!" I shouted.

I backtracked and grabbed hold of his arm so he'd walk faster.

"Pinky, look what you've done," he yelled. "You made me step on a crack. Now we're going to have bad luck."

I needed all the luck I could get to solve this mystery.

The rest of the way to the train station I made sure not to step on any cracks!

Chapter Twelve

We could hear the roar of the elevated trains above us as we got closer to the subway station. Avi, Lucy, and I hiked up the stairs to the platform where Madame Olga was waiting for us.

"Look what I brought, darlings," she said, holding up a shopping bag. "It's a little nosh in case you get hungry."

I took one look at the bag and thought she must have packed enough snacks to feed all the kids in Brooklyn.

"We'll take the W train to West 8th Street in

Coney Island," Madame Olga told us. "From there we'll walk to the aquarium."

Since it was Sunday, there weren't too many people waiting to catch a train. Even the kiosk that sold water and magazines was closed. A little girl in a stroller was eating a bagel, and it reminded me that I hadn't had breakfast.

Just as I was about to ask Madame Olga to share her bag of snacks, a man in a gray jacket walked over to us. He looked familiar. "Madame Olga! What a lovely coincidence!"

"Mr. Federman!" exclaimed Madame Olga. "Good morning! Darlings, this is Mr. Federman from the Jewish Museum." She introduced the three of us, and he shook our hands.

"Of course, your parents own the Lotus Blossom Restaurant," Mr. Federman said, smiling at Lucy. "And I remember seeing your friends there." He winked at Avi.

"Pinky is a detective and I'm her helper," Avi declared. "We're solving a mystery."

I elbowed Avi in the ribs. This case was top secret, and I wanted it to stay that way.

"Well, that's very exciting," Mr. Federman said. "And what is it you're working on, might I ask?"

Luckily, Avi didn't get a chance to answer Mr. Federman because at that moment our train pulled into the station. It came to a screeching stop in front of us, and the doors slid open.

We hurried inside and found a bench along the wall that was big enough for all of us to sit together.

"Sit here, Mr. Federman," Madame Olga said. "There's plenty of room."

"Where are you and these charming children going?" he asked.

Avi told Mr. Federman we were going to the New York Aquarium. "We're looking for the Hat Lady," he said. "So Lucy doesn't have to move."

"The New York Aquarium!" exclaimed Mr. Federman. "How lovely. I haven't been there in so long."

"Why don't you join us?" Madame Olga suggested.

Mr. Federman beamed. "I'd be delighted."

I looked out the window . . . and saw Joe the Waiter! He hopped onto our train just as the doors were about to close!

Chapter Thirteen

The train came to a stop at the Coney Island Station. When we stepped out onto the platform, I looked around for Joe the Waiter, but I didn't see him. Maybe he'd stayed on the train.

When we got to the aquarium entrance, Mr. Federman was first in line to buy tickets. "Three children and two adults, please," he said, winking at us. "This will be my treat."

Madame Olga leaned over and whispered in my ear, "Such a mensch! A good man."

We thanked Mr. Federman. Then Madame

Olga asked the ticket seller how to get to the Seaside Restaurant.

"Sorry, the restaurant has been closed for renovations," she said. "It'll reopen tomorrow afternoon."

I groaned. Our biggest lead had dried up!

Madame Olga said, "Not to worry, darlings. We can still enjoy the aquarium."

The ticket seller suggested we start at Conservation Hall. "It's where we have the largest collection of fish from all over the world," she said.

We walked over to Conservation Hall. Inside were aquariums filled with hundreds of amazing, colorful fish.

Madame Olga was across the room from us, standing in front of a huge tank. "Over here, darlings," she called out. "Look, I found the carp. On Passover, Lucy, we use it to make gefilte fish."

We all crowded around and watched as a school of carp swam in and out of seaweed.

"There's an ancient Chinese legend that says carp leap over waterfalls and change into dragons!" Lucy told us.

"There's no such thing as a dragon," Avi said. "Only Komodo dragons are real, and they live on an island in the ocean and eat snakes and rats."

Lucy didn't seem to mind how obnoxious Avi was acting. "Carp also bring riches and success to the people who own them," she added cheerfully.

I might have to ask for a fish tank filled with carp next Hanukkah.

Avi put his nose close to the tank's glass. "The fish don't have anything to play with," he said.

I shrugged. "They're having fun swimming in and out of the rock formations."

"But Pinky, the fish in the restaurant's aquarium had a toy in their tank."

Mr. Federman quickly jumped in. "I think the sea lion show is about to start," he said. "We don't want to miss that, do we?"

I looked over at Mr. Federman. His face was as green as the seaweed in the carp's tank!

Chapter Fourteen

We walked out of Conservation Hall just as a voice on the PA system announced that the sea lion show would start in twenty minutes. "That's lots of time!" said Avi. "Let's go back—"

"What if we look at some of the other outdoor exhibits instead?" suggested Mr. Federman.

At the Touch Pool, Avi dipped his hands into the water. "I touched a stingray!" he said proudly. "It was slimy and yucky."

Next we stopped and watched the penguins. They waddled around on the edge of the pool, and then they dove in.

"Okay, now it really *is* time for the sea lion show," Mr. Federman said, looking at his watch.

We walked over to the Aquatheater, where the show was being held. Tall metal bleachers surrounded a large swimming pool. We climbed up the steep stairs and sat down in our seats.

Lucy, Madame Olga, and Avi were on one side of me. And on my other side was Mr. Federman. Madame Olga leaned over and handed each of us a sandwich wrapped in waxed paper. "Eat up before the show starts. If you want more, I have."

As I happily munched on my salami sandwich, I realized this was the perfect time to interview Mr. Federman about the case. "Do you go to the Lotus Blossom a lot?" I asked him.

"I've been there a few times since it opened," he said. "Do you and your family eat there often?"

"Lucy's parents own it, so we like it. The food tastes good, but Avi doesn't like to eat the vegetables."

Mr. Federman stared at me. "What happens to his leftovers?"

"We take them home, and then I hide them in the refrigerator," Avi chimed in.

My mom still hadn't found Avi's leftovers, and by now they were probably growing green hairy mold.

I shot Avi an irritated look. How was I supposed to interview this witness properly if my brother interrupted me?

Mr. Federman looked as if he wanted to say something else, but at that moment, music blasted, and the show began.

A trainer in waterproof coveralls and rubber boots stepped out onto a platform suspended over the swimming pool. "Good morning, folks," she said. "My name is Martha, and this is Bernie."

Bernie was a brown sea lion. He waddled over to Martha. Then she bent down and shook his flipper.

Martha asked Bernie if he wanted to go for a swim. He bobbed his head and slid into the pool.

We all cheered as we watched Bernie swim in circles.

And when Martha blew her whistle, he climbed out of the pool and waddled back over to her. "Take a bow, Bernie," Martha said and rewarded him with a fish.

Next Martha asked for a volunteer from the audience. "Who would like to perform with Bernie?"

"Oh, pick me!" Avi shouted, waving his hand. "I like all animals, but I love sea lions the best."

"She doesn't see you, Avi," I said. "We're too high up."

Lucy and I also tried waving, but Martha gave the nod to a man in the front row.

The man hesitated, but then he got up from his seat and walked over to Martha and Bernie.

She whispered something in the man's ear. Then she leaned down and said, "Bernie, let's see what you have for this nice gentleman."

The man bent down, and Bernie planted a kiss on his cheek.

Everyone in the audience laughed, except for me. I was too busy digging through my backpack for my binoculars.

I focused them on the man Bernie had kissed. "Just as I thought," I said to myself. "It's Joe the Waiter!"

Chapter Fifteen

At the end of the show, I grabbed Lucy's hand and together we ran down the bleacher steps.

"You look for him over there," I said, pointing to the row of seats where Joe had been sitting. "I'll go question Martha."

I had to find Joe the Waiter and ask him why he was showing up everywhere we went.

Bernie was swimming in the pool while Martha put away props from the show.

"Excuse me," I said. "Do you know where the man you picked from the audience went?"

Bernie hopped out of the pool. He must've thought it was showtime.

"The show's over, Bernie," Martha told him. "Now, who is it you're looking for, young lady?"

"The man who was just here. You know, Bernie gave him a kiss."

"Oh, that man. I'm not sure where he went. I'm sorry I can't help you."

Martha walked away carrying the bucket of fish, with Bernie following close behind.

Lucy hurried over. "I looked everywhere, but I didn't see Joe the Waiter. Did you find out anything?"

"No—I think Bernie knows where he is, but he's not talking!"

"He probably just went to work, Pinky. The restaurant opens soon."

I had to come up with another plan since the only thing I learned at the aquarium was how to get a sea lion to do tricks.

"Lucy, do you think we could have dinner at your parents' restaurant tonight?"

"Of course!"

Great, now I just had to find Madame Olga and tell her the plan.

Madame Olga, Mr. Federman, and Avi were waiting for us outside the Aquatheater.

"Nu, where did you two disappear all of a sudden?" Madame Olga asked.

Lucy spoke up first. "My parents invited everyone to have dinner at the restaurant tonight, and it's their treat."

Madame Olga handed me her cell phone. "First, Pinky, you'll call your mother. See if it's all right by her."

I called home, and Grandma Phyllis answered the phone. "What, more Chinese food?" she said. "Avi's leftovers are still sitting in the refrigerator. Wait, I'll go see if they're good."

"Grandma, listen . . ."

"It'll just take me a minute. Don't be so impatient, Pinky." After a few seconds she got back to me. "Pinky, something's not right . . ."

"I know, Grandma, throw them away. Avi won't care. I have to go now. Bye."

I handed the phone back to Madame Olga. "Grandma Phyllis said we can go to the restaurant," I fibbed.

"Would you like to join us, Mr. Federman?" asked Madame Olga.

Mr. Federman smiled, but he had an odd look in his eyes. "I'd love to."

Avi took me aside. "Pinky, why are we going there again?"

"I want to question Joe the Waiter, and I'm hoping the Hat Lady will show up."

"*T-i-x-e* is this way," Avi said, reading the aquarium's exit sign backwards.

"Stop doing that," I yelled. "It's so annoying!"

"*Y-a-k-o, Y-k-n-i-p*," Avi said, with a sly grin.

"Let's take a shortcut through the parking lot," Mr. Federman suggested. "We'll get to the train station faster that way."

As we headed across the parking lot, I noticed a bakery truck parked in the space reserved for deliveries. Suddenly the hairs on my head stood on end. The name on the truck was Mazer's Bakery!

Chapter Sixteen

We all rode the subway back to our neighborhood and walked to the Lotus Blossom Kosher Chinese Restaurant.

Mazer's Bakery was next door, but since it was Sunday night, there was a Closed sign on the window.

I peeked inside and saw bare shelves and empty display cases.

Lucy came up behind me. "What are you looking for?" she said.

"I wanted to ask Mrs. Mazer about the delivery truck parked at the aquarium, but no one's here."

"Let's go, I'm hungry," Avi complained, tugging on my arm.

"Wait," I said. "Don't you think it would be weird for the aquarium to order baked goods from Mazer's *and* from the Hat Lady's place? Wouldn't they just get everything from one business?"

"What are you getting at, Pinky?" asked Lucy.

"What if the place the Hat Lady works for—the place that makes your fortune cookies—is actually Mazer's?"

Lucy looked puzzled. "But the boxes of cookies said it was the Rezam Fortune Cookie Company, not Mazer's."

"Hey!" Avi shouted. "*M-a-z-e-r* spelled backwards is Rezam."

Wow! That made sense, though I hated to admit he was right.

"Yoo-hoo!" called Madame Olga up ahead. "What's keeping you, darlings?"

"Let's keep this to ourselves for the moment," I whispered to Lucy and Avi. "We still need proof."

We walked into the restaurant, and Mrs. Wong immediately led us toward our table. But I hung back in the entryway.

I walked over to the fish tank, pressed my nose against the glass, and watched as one of the fish pecked at the gravel in the bottom of the tank.

Something Avi had said was bugging me . . .

Aha!

Once I'd found what I was looking for, I rushed over to join the others at a large round table close to the entryway. Before I could say anything, Avi reached into his backpack and pulled out his hand sanitizer. "Who wants to use this?" he said, unscrewing the cap.

"Don't use it all up, Avi," I warned. "It belongs to Grandma Phyllis."

No sooner had those words left my mouth than Grandma Phyllis walked into the restaurant and marched over to our table!

Chapter Seventeen

"Can someone please tell me the meaning of this?" she demanded, holding a white takeout container.

"I can explain, Grandma," Avi stammered. "I didn't want to eat the vegetables, so I put it in the back of the refrigerator where Mom wouldn't find it."

Grandma Phyllis looked at Avi as if he was a Martian. "What leftovers, Avi? Here's what I'm talking about."

She reached into the takeout container and pulled out a gold Kiddush cup!

Mr. Federman lunged for the cup. "I believe

that belongs to me," he said. "I'm so glad you found it!"

Grandma Phyllis took a few steps backward. "I beg your pardon, sir, but isn't this the Kiddush cup that was taken from the Jewish Museum last week?"

"Perhaps your granddaughter knows something about that, ma'am," Mr. Federman said. "I believe *she* was the one who took that container from this restaurant and brought it home."

Avi jumped up from his seat. "You're mean, Mr. Federman! My sister didn't put a Kiddush cup in my leftovers."

Avi sat back down, and his arm bumped the open bottle of hand sanitizer. Smelly goo spread across the table and dripped down onto the floor.

Joe the Waiter appeared out of nowhere. "Hands up, Federman!" he barked. "You're under arrest for robbing the Jewish Museum."

Mr. Federman looked surprised. "You've got the wrong man, officer!" he said. "I had nothing to do with the robbery."

"Nice try," Officer Joe said. "But your accomplice, Mrs. Wong, gave you up."

Mr. Federman bolted out of his seat and tried

to make a run for it—but he slipped on the hand sanitizer that puddled on the floor.

In one swift move Mr. Federman slid feetfirst into the restaurant's aquarium. Glass shattered. Gallons of water and fish spilled out onto the floor.

Avi grabbed a water glass from the table and tried to save the fish that were flopping around.

Lucy turned to me. "Pinky, is it always this exciting when you're on a case?"

Madame Olga fanned herself with a menu. "Oy! I'm a little farklempt," she said. "Who knew he was a no-goodnik?"

Officer Joe grabbed hold of Mr. Federman by the seat of his pants and slapped on a pair of handcuffs.

"Wait a minute," I shouted. "There's one more piece of unfinished business."

I waded through shards of glass and puddles of water until I found what I was looking for.

"I think you'll want this for evidence," I said, handing Officer Joe a silver Torah pointer. "It was hidden in the fish tank."

Suddenly the smoke alarm went off. A woman wearing a floppy hat and sunglasses ran out of the kitchen with Chef Wong chasing her.

"You made trouble for the restaurant!" he shouted. "I'll turn you into moo goo gai pan!"

"That's her," Avi cried. "It's the Hat Lady!"

The woman stopped in her tracks and looked around at the chaos. "Hey, what's going on here?"

"Welcome to the party, Mrs. Mazer," I said. "You have some explaining to do!"

BOO-HOO! A face like yours makes a ghost scream

Chapter Eighteen

The next Sunday, Lucy's parents invited my family to be their guests at the Lotus Blossom Kosher Chinese Restaurant again. Our meal would be their treat since Avi and I had helped save their business.

Mrs. Wong was gone, but Lucy's mom and dad were waiting to greet us in the entryway.

"Welcome, Pinky," Mrs. Chang said. "It's an honor to have a famous detective eating dinner with us tonight."

"Thank you, Mrs. Chang," I said. "I'm glad I

could help out because now Lucy won't have to move away."

"And you can borrow my sweatshirt anytime you want!" Lucy added.

"Are you going to get a new fish tank?" Avi asked Mr. Chang.

"Yes, we are, Avi. And you can help us pick out some new fish." Mrs. Chang showed us to our table. "Enjoy your dinner," she said. "Someone will be here shortly to take your order."

"Pinky, will Officer Joe be our waiter?" Avi wanted to know. "I really liked him."

"He can't because he's busy being a police officer," I said. "But he can still be our friend."

"I'm curious, Pinky," Mom said. "Why was the Torah pointer in the fish tank?"

"Mrs. Wong was hiding it there until Mr. Federman was ready to sell it. They figured no one would think to look for a stolen artifact there."

I had to give Avi credit. He was the one who'd first noticed there was something besides fish in the restaurant's fish tank. But I was the one who figured out it was stolen goods.

"Their plan worked like this," I went on. "Mr.

Federman was in charge of the special exhibit, so he knew how valuable the Kiddush cup and the Torah pointer were. He could've just stolen them himself, but he was worried about getting caught. So he had Mrs. Wong do the stealing for him. Then she brought the stolen goods to the restaurant. Mr. Federman was supposed to come here to eat, sneak them out of the restaurant, and sell them one at a time. Then they'd split the profits."

"So how did the Kiddush cup wind up in Avi's leftovers?" Grandma Phyllis said.

I explained, "When we ate here two weeks ago, Mr. Federman was about to smuggle the cup out of the restaurant inside a takeout container. When there was all that commotion with the mouse, I accidentally grabbed Mr. Federman's takeout container instead of Avi's."

"Pinky, what about Mrs. Mazer?" Mom asked. "What did she have to do with the burglary?"

"Nothing! She was just trying to put the restaurant out of business so she could expand her bakery into this space. That's why she brought in a mouse, set off the smoke alarm, and put those awful fortunes in the fortune cookies she made for the restaurant."

Suddenly a voice behind me said, "Can I get you something to drink, bubeleh?"

I looked up and saw Madame Olga. She had a pad and pencil in her hand. The restaurant's new server was waiting to take our order!

Chapter Nineteen

"Nu?" Madame Olga said, looking around at our surprised faces. "A psychic can't have a second job?"

I thought it was great to have a psychic waitress. This way she already knew that I didn't like brussels sprouts.

After we were done eating, Madame Olga brought us our fortune cookies. "Here, darlings, these are from a new bakery. Not like the ones from Mazer's."

"What's going to happen to Mrs. Mazer?" Avi asked. "Did Officer Joe put her in jail?"

"My parents decided not to press charges," Lucy said. "Mrs. Mazer said that she's sorry for all the trouble she caused and that she's going to open a new bakery in Queens. Now my parents are planning to buy the old bakery building and expand the restaurant."

"Read your fortunes already," Madame Olga said. "Let's see if they're so good they'll put me out of business."

Avi went first. He cleared his throat. *"A new pet will come into your life.* Yes! That means I'm getting one of Oy Vey's kittens!"

Dad rolled his eyes. "We'll see about that," he said under his breath.

Next, Mom read her fortune. *"Laughter is the music of a happy heart."* She looked around the table. "That's very true. And my heart is very happy tonight."

My dad read his fortune. *"Be thankful, for riches will soon be yours.* That's a great one," he declared. "Now I only hope it comes true."

Then it was Grandma Phyllis's turn. *"Your return home will be delayed.* That's amazing," she said. "Who knew I was planning to stay in Brooklyn a little longer?"

Oh no, I thought. *Now I'll be stuck with Avi in my room forever!*

"Okay, Pinky bubeleh," Madame Olga said. "Let's hear your fortune."

I pulled the slip of paper out from my fortune cookie and read, *"Excitement and intrigue follow wherever you go."*

I liked the sound of that. Sooner or later someone will need my help, and I, Penina "Pinky" Bloom, Brooklyn's greatest kid detective, will get to solve another case.

When we got home from the restaurant, I ran into my room. D.J. was prowling around on my desk.

I watched as he lifted his paw and pressed the alarm button on my clock. "You're a rascally cat!" I scolded him.

I thought for a minute. Then I went to find Avi. "Um, I have something to tell you," I said. "I guess it was D.J. who set off my alarm a few days ago—not you. Sorry I blamed you for it."

"That's okay, Pinky. I knew you wouldn't be mad at me forever."

I guess having a little brother isn't so bad after all.

About the Author

Judy Press studied fine arts at Syracuse University and earned a masters in art education from the University of Pittsburgh. She is the creator of a dozen award-winning children's art activity books and early reader chapter books. A grandmother to ten, Press lives in Pittsburgh.

About the Illustrator

Originally from Ireland, Erica-Jane Waters credits her imagination to her childhood there and its wealth of folklore and fairy tales. She has been writing and illustrating children's books for over twenty years and uses a mixture of traditional techniques and digital work to create her art. Waters lives in a 370-year-old tumbledown cottage in deepest, darkest Northamptonshire in England with her husband and two children.